Also by J.R. Hardin

THE KUDZU MONSTERS
Published in June 2010

Coming in spring of 2011
KUDZU MONSTERS VERSUS
THE CREEPER HORDE

BOOK TWO

KALVIN THE KUDZU MONSTER

J.R. HARDIN

iUniverse, Inc.
New York   Bloomington

Kalvin the Kudzu Monster

iUniverse books may be ordered through booksellers or by contacting:

iUniverse
1663 Liberty Drive
Bloomington, IN 47403
www.iuniverse.com
1-800-Authors (1-800-288-4677)

Because of the dynamic nature of the Internet, any Web addresses or links contained in this book may have changed since publication and may no longer be valid. The views expressed in this work are solely those of the author and do not necessarily reflect the views of the publisher, and the publisher hereby disclaims any responsibility for them.

ISBN: 978-1-4502-5764-0 (sc)
ISBN: 978-1-4502-5765-7 (ebook)

Printed in the United States of America

iUniverse rev. date: 9/23/2010

Table of Contents

INTRODUCTION

◡

My story is about a young kudzu monster named Kalvin. In my first book, *THE KUDZU MONSTERS*, I explained how kudzu monsters were formed by kudzu vines completely covering a tree. I gave a brief history about kudzu and how it spread rapidly throughout the southeastern states of America. Here are some additional facts about kudzu.

The kudzu vines produce a sweet-smelling flower that blooms in Georgia from July until September or October. The wisteria-shaped flowers are around six inches long and vary in color but are usually red, or red at the base and purple or blue near the end of the flower. The sweet blossoms can be smelt hundreds of feet away. In my books only the female monsters produce flowers.

Because of the vine's rapid growth it's known by such names (in the south) as "foot-a-night vine" and "the vine that ate the south."

The vines spread by runners that root at the nodes to form new plants, but they can also spread by seed pods. These pods may not germinate for several years. This can result in the reappearance of vines that were thought to be destroyed. The roots can grow to a diameter of several inches and to a depth of ten feet.

Kudzu takes four to ten years to kill with repeated herbicide treatments. This is why the vines cover more than seven million acres of land in the southeastern states.

ACKNOWLEDGMENTS

I wish to thank my sister, Betty Hertenstein, for editing my books. Without her skills my stories wouldn't flow as smoothly and would be riddled with mistakes.

CHAPTER ONE

~

WALK ABOUT

Kalvin paced back and forth.

"I'm not saying I'll be gone for a year. I just want to explore the forest on my own until winter starts."

"You're only eleven years old," said Kitty.

"I'm eleven and a half, Mom. I'm nearly eleven feet tall and weigh over seven hundred pounds. I can take care of myself."

"You explore the forest nearly every day," Kitty replied.

"I want to explore the deep forest. I want to discover new places and see different things."

Kitty looked to Kalvin's father. "Kleatus, don't you think Kalvin is too young for a long trip by himself?"

"I made a similar trip when I was about his age," Kleatus responded. "There's not much that can harm him."

"I won't be gone that long," added Kalvin. "I'll head back when my leaves start falling."

"All right, Kalvin, you can go," Kitty sighed. "Be extra careful and watch out for deer hunters. They're all over the forest this time of year."

"Some of those hunters shoot at any movement in the woods," Kleatus chimed in. "I've been shot three times in my fifty-one years."

"Wow! You're an old kudzu monster."

"Fifty-one isn't old for us," Kitty jumped in. "Our friend Karl is over sixty and an old monster named Karrie is around a hundred."

"I really don't know how long we live," said Kleatus. "No kudzu monster has ever died of old age. Fire, lightning and falling from cliffs are about the only things that can kill us."

The next night Kalvin hugged his parents and his little sister, Kandi. His squirrel friend, Squiggy, came out of his burrow to tell Kalvin good-bye.

"Remember, Kalvin, when winter is here the squirrels will be in their burrows and won't be around to warn you of danger in the forest," Kleatus cautioned him.

"Don't worry, Dad. I've been roaming the forest for over eleven years and I've never been injured."

"You've had friends to warn you," added Kitty. "Heed his warning about taking extra care. Don't use the trail too often. Make your way through the forest."

Kalvin smiled and waved bye to everyone. *If I don't use the trail I'll be lucky to make one mile an hour*, he thought. *Only a few leaves have changed color. There are still plenty of squirrels and forest friends to warn me of danger.*

Kalvin's tentacle feet pushed and pulled him slowly through the forest. *I don't think there's any danger of running into hunters late at night. I'll use the trail at night and travel in the forest during the day.*

Kalvin continued to travel in this fashion for several days. Late one day he found a small waterfall. *This is a pleasant spot. I've been walking for three days and nights. This would be a good spot to rest and feed. Mom and Dad are worried needlessly. I've been pushing through the forest with the trail in sight and haven't seen a single human. If I keep my eyes and ear slots open for danger, I think it'll be okay to use the trail during the day.*

The next day Kalvin was pushing along the trail when he heard a noise that sounded like several chainsaws running. The roar grew louder. He moved to the edge of the trail and stopped.

Suddenly, a trail bike popped over the hill and into the air. A second biker was a few yards behind him. The bikes sailed through the air and landed on the trail in front of him. Spewing dirt into the air, they roared past as a third biker raced over the hill. This biker landed partly on the trail and partly on one of Kalvin's foot tentacles. The back end of the bike swiped Kalvin ripping some kudzu vines from his tree-trunk body. The bike continued past and plowed into a small tree. The teenage driver was thrown through the air into a large bush. Kalvin saw that the teenager's biker buddies had stopped and were watching their friend.

Kalvin held still even though his foot tentacle was throbbing with pain. He watched the biker get up, dust off his leather jacket and pick up his bike.

"I'm okay," he hollered to his friends.

He doesn't seem to be injured. That's more than I can say for my foot, and my side stings a little.

The other bikers waited for their fallen friend to start his bike again and resumed their reckless race.

Kalvin examined his wounds. His side looked okay but some of the hide on his foot had been ripped off. Thick green fluid was seeping from a small gash on top of his wounded foot tentacle. As he began pushing and pulling deeper into the woods, Kalvin held onto trees with his four arm tentacles to take some weight off his injured foot.

Well, my foot still works okay. I'll move away from the trail and rest until dark. I guess I'll go back to traveling in the woods during the daylight hours.

Kalvin rested until after midnight before he renewed his journey. The new moon offered little light, but he could see very well in the dark. His foot hurt when he moved but had stopped bleeding. He hoped it would feel better the more he used it and that it wouldn't start bleeding again.

Kudzu monsters can't bend very well, so he had to strain to see his foot. He stopped several times during the night to rest and to examine his wound.

The sun has risen and I only covered two miles last night. I'll rest here until afternoon. It'll give my foot time to heal some more.

All of a sudden Kalvin heard something crashing through the forest. He twisted to his right as a deer burst through the brush and ran toward him. The deer darted to the left and crossed in front of him. A rifle thundered and Kalvin felt a sharp pain in his side.

CHAPTER TWO

❧

THE STORM

Kalvin remained in his frozen position. The deer bounded away and the forest grew silent. *Good grief, in just a few days of walking I've had a trail bike run over my foot and a hunter shoot me.* His side was throbbing, but he couldn't check the wound until the hunter left.

A couple of minutes later a squirrel scurried across the ground to Kalvin and climbed up to his ear slot.

"Don't move," the squirrel told him. "There's a hunter behind you on a tree stand."

"Thank you," Kalvin replied. "You're a little late with the warning. The hunter already shot me. He hit me on my right side. Would you do me a favor and tell me how bad the wound looks?"

"No worry," answered the squirrel. "I'll pop down there and have a look."

The squirrel climbed down to the wound. Several minutes passed by without his return.

"Mister Squirrel," whispered Kalvin, "are you still here?"

"I'm right here," answered the squirrel. "What do you want?"

"You were going to tell me how bad the bullet wound looked."

"Oh, yeah, the wound; the bullet only scratched you," answered the squirrel. "I'll tell you when the hunter leaves."

"I would appreciate that," replied Kalvin.

Kalvin remained very still for nearly an hour. His feeder roots burrowed into the rich forest soil and nourished his bruised body. The bullet wound still stung and he wondered what the squirrel considered a scratch.

Kalvin heard something climbing down the tree, followed by rustling in the bushes behind him. He waited for the squirrel to report the hunter was gone. Several minutes passed and the squirrel remained silent.

"Mister Squirrel, has the hunter left?" whispered Kalvin.

The squirrel didn't answer.

"Mister Squirrel, are you there?"

When he didn't hear an answer, Kalvin assumed the squirrel must have forgotten about the hunter and left.

Kalvin began slowly turning in the direction of the hunter's tree stand. It was empty and the hunter was gone.

Squirrels, I love them, thought Kalvin. *But some have the attention span of a butterfly. I wish they were all like Squiggy. He's the smartest squirrel I know. Squiggy doesn't forget things like most squirrels.* He sure wished Squiggy were with him. But Squiggy was busy gathering nuts for the winter. He even missed his little sister, Kandi, tagging along behind him.

A couple of days passed. Kalvin felt good. His wounds didn't hurt and he was exploring new territory. Most of the leaves had started changing color. He'd have to head home in a couple of weeks. *All in all, it hasn't been a bad trip -- a couple of mishaps, but nothing too serious.*

Just then, a raccoon ambled up to him and said, "Old Scar is headed your way!"

"Who is Old Scar?" Kalvin asked, but the raccoon hurried away and climbed up a tall tulip tree.

His question was answered when a big black bear with a long scar across his snout lumbered into sight. *The bear won't attack me if I don't move. Oh, great, he's headed straight toward me.* Old Scar stopped at a maple tree beside him. The bear stood on his hind legs and raked his claws up and down the tree. Bark crumbled to the ground and sap flowed from the scarred tree.

Oh, no, the bear is marking his territory. I hope he doesn't decide to mark me.

Old Scar turned and trotted over to Kalvin. He'd never heard of a bear marking a kudzu monster before. All their vines made it harder to claw through.

The big bear sniffed Kalvin. He turned his rear end to Kalvin and began backing up. The beast pushed his bottom on Kalvin and began moving his rump up and down.

Terrific, thought Kalvin, *I'm being used as a scratching post for a bear's butt.* He had to hold onto a tree to keep from toppling over. Having satisfied his itch, the bear waddled away.

Kalvin looked at the cloudy sky and hoped it would rain today. He could do with a bath after that. Later that day it looked like Kalvin might get his wish. Gray clouds formed and a steady rain began to fall. Unfortunately, most of the rain was landing on the tree leaves above him.

I need to climb to the top of the hill where the trees are thin if I want a good shower. As he pushed up the hill, a light rain began to wash over him. He glanced around and noticed the squirrels had gone into their burrows and the birds had flown to their nests. The sky had turned darker and distant thunder boomed. A storm was coming! He saw a flash of lightning.

I'd better leave the higher ground before I'm struck by lightning. Lightning and fire were the two things that scared kudzu monsters the most. Kalvin hurried down the hill as the wind roared through the trees and rain poured down. Leaves and small limbs fell from the trees. The day grew darker and thunder shook the ground. Kalvin was blinded for a moment by a flash of lightning. Water splashed against him and flowed past in small streams. Holding onto trees to keep from loosing his footing, Kalvin raced down the hill.

Suddenly, there was a bright flash. He felt heat and heard a loud crack as the lightning hit something close. A jolt of electricity knocked him backwards. He grabbed onto two small trees to keep from falling. From his leaning position he saw the top of a poplar tree crashing through the branches toward him.

CHAPTER THREE

~

THE DAM

Kalvin turned loose of the small trees as the top of the large poplar struck where his tentacles had been. He fell flat on his back as a branch of the tree top just missed an arm and plowed into the earth.

Wow, that was close, thought Kalvin. He wasn't hurt, but he was penned under the tree top. He could probably lift the tree top, but it was too heavy for him to cast off. As he pushed forward to slide from under the tree, the base of his trunk struck a large rock. Kalvin pushed with his feet, but couldn't budge it. He pushed himself backwards with his arms to try lifting the tree top with his feet tentacles.

In a short time a foot tentacle touched the tree limb. Only the top two of his eight feet tentacles were able to push up on the tree top. He pushed upward but couldn't lift the tree top high enough to get free.

How am I going to get out from under this tree top? Maybe I can angle my body and slide past that big rock. Bending forward slightly, he lifted his body with his arms. He angled his upper body to the left, pushed forward and tried sliding to the right of the rock. Although the rain had made the ground slippery, Kalvin had to pull on trees and shrubs to slide past the rock.

Well, I'm not penned under the tree top, but I need to get on my feet again. He saw a low tree limb and pushed under it. His arms began to pull up while he pushed backward with three feet tentacles that touched

9

the ground. He had pulled up several feet when his feet slipped on the muddy slope. Kalvin slid down the hill and was on his back again.

I need to brace my feet against something before I pull with my arms. He lifted up and saw a rock down the hill where he could brace his feet and a nearby tree to help him up. Kalvin scooted toward it and a few minutes later he was standing on his feet.

That was quite an ordeal. I better hang onto trees going down this slippery slope. I don't want to end up on my back again.

The rain continued, but the lightning was dying down as Kalvin came to the bottom of the hill, but another hill loomed before him. A stream flowed between the hills.

I'll follow the stream and see where it leads me.

The sun had set and the cloud cover made the night much darker. As Kalvin followed the flow, the stream grew wider and ran into a man-made lake. Kalvin circled the lake until he found the stream again.

Eventually the stream flowed under a wooden bridge and a small bank was in front of him. Kalvin pushed to the top of the bank and found a road leading to the bridge.

The rain continued to pour as Kalvin crossed the bridge. The lights of several houses glowed along a bank between the road and the rising stream. Kalvin saw people moving about in their homes.

Kandi would enjoy this. She loves to watch humans.

A gush of water flowed down the stream making it rise several inches.

I wonder what caused that. There's a trail on the other side of the bridge. I'll follow it back up to the lake.

When he reached the tall bank that held back the water in the lake, he saw a drain pipe near the bottom that let the water flow from the lake. But water was gushing out to the left side of the pipe and from a gap at the top of the bank. The break was getting wider as water poured through it.

If the dam breaks, those houses could be washed away. I've got to do something!

Kalvin went down to the stream and pulled on a large rock. The mud made a sucking noise as he lifted it up. He easily carried the rock even though it weighed a couple of hundred pounds. Kalvin's upper arms tossed the boulder into the break at the top. Water flowed over the rock, but the break wasn't as deep.

He went back for a second rock and then another. He noticed the gap wasn't getting any deeper, but was growing wider. More water flowed through the break as the stream continued to rise. *I'm fighting a losing battle. The break is growing faster than I can plug it. I've got to warn the humans of the danger!*

Kalvin hurried back to the houses as fast as his feet could push and pull on the slippery trail. When he arrived at the bridge, most of the house lights were off.

Many of the humans must be in bed, but I see a man sitting in a chair. I need to get his attention.

Kalvin picked up a small stone and threw it on the wooden deck at the back of the house. The man looked toward the deck, but he didn't get out of his chair. Kalvin pulled up a five-foot bush and hurled it onto the deck. This time the man jumped up and ran to his deck. Then he went back in the house, put on his raincoat and walked onto the deck with a flashlight.

The man shined the light on the bush and stared at it for a minute, but turned back to the house without looking at the growing stream.

"The dam's breaking!" hollered Kalvin.

"What," the man answered. "Who's out there? What did you say about the dam?"

"The dam's breaking," Kalvin shouted. "Look at the water."

The man shined a flashlight at Kalvin and around the woods looking for the man that shouted at him. Finally he looked at the water and ran back into the house. Kalvin was glad the man understood him. The slow deep speech of a kudzu monster was hard for a human to follow.

The man screamed, "Wake up the dam's breaking!" He ran outside to a small building. He unlocked the building and ran inside. Soon a siren was screeching and lights came on in all the houses. The families began getting into their cars with their pets and a little luggage. As the cars began to pull onto the road, a great rumbling noise came from up stream.

Oh, no, thought Kalvin, *the dam has broken!*

CHAPTER FOUR

WASHED AWAY

Kalvin pushed up the hill to higher ground as the roaring continued to grow. He had climbed several feet higher when water taller than a man's head surged down the creek. The raging water swept past Kalvin and crashed into the first house. The back deck was torn from the house and tossed into the next house. A lone car, although clear of the water, was trapped in the driveway by a fallen tree.

The water splashed over Kalvin's feet tentacles, but went unnoticed as he watched a man climb out of the car. The man hurried to the passenger side and helped a woman out who was carrying a small child in her arms. A young girl climbed out behind her. The man assisted the woman up the driveway as the girl clung to the back of his coat. He lifted the woman over the fallen tree and reached back for the girl.

Suddenly, the tree slid a couple of feet downhill knocking the man to the ground and the girl onto the muddy bank.

"Daddy, help! I'm slipping." yelled the girl.

The stunned man remained on the ground. Kalvin moved along the bank toward the girl.

"Steve, get up!" the woman screamed. "Beth is sliding toward the water."

The man groaned and tried to get to his feet. The lower half of the girl was in the water as she clung to a tree stump. As Kalvin waded into the water, he wrapped his arm tentacles around trees to keep from being washed downstream. He pulled from tree to tree as he closed the distance between himself and the girl. Kalvin glanced up the hill. The man was sitting up, but his head was bleeding. Kalvin was only a hundred feet from them, but in the storm no one had noticed him.

Beth held onto the stump and started to climb to her feet. She stood up and tried walking up the hill. Just then she slipped and fell backwards into the water.

Kalvin pushed away from the trees and plunged into the water. He steered his body with his arms until he was headed downstream feet first. Kalvin heard the woman crying and screaming for Steve. He could see Beth bobbing in the water as she struggled to keep afloat. Using his arms like oars, he turned his body at an angle to better see Beth. It wasn't long before he reached her. She reached out with a hand and caught hold of one of his feet tentacles. He put his left lower arm beneath Beth and slowly pushed her up onto his body.

Beth sat on Kalvin and held onto his feet. Her legs hung down his sides with her feet dragging in the water.

I need to find a spot to put her on shore, with a gentle bank slope and trees to help her climb the bank.

He pushed through the water with his two right arms and moved closer to the left bank.

The water flow is slower away from the middle of the stream.

Kalvin spotted a gentle slope and steered toward it. He grabbed a tree limb and pulled to the bank. Moving his right arms underwater, he rowed backwards to remain stationary.

She should be able to jump off of me and grab onto a tree.

Kalvin waited a minute for her to climb ashore, but she just sat there hanging onto his feet. He reached around her waist with his lower left tentacle and picked her up.

"Help me!" Beth screamed.

Kalvin set her on the bank as she continued to cry for help.

"Beth, where are you?" called a man's voice and a flashlight shone from the road above.

"Daddy, I'm here!" Beth cried back. "A giant snake is after me!"

The man hurried to Beth, hugged her and they began to climb the bank.

When they're out of sight, I'll pull up and climb out of this flood.

Kalvin was just thinking everything would be okay, when something large loomed behind him.

Oh, my stars, it's the bridge I crossed earlier!

A wooden beam slid over him and dug into the muddy bank. The structure twisted and Kalvin's kudzu vines entangled with the bridge. Kalvin was spun to the middle of the stream. Kudzu vines tore from his arms and chest as he tried to pull free from the wooden mass. The bridge rolled and Kalvin was pushed under water. He wasn't worried about drowning, because kudzu monsters don't have lungs, but he scraped the rocks at the bottom of the stream.

I have to get free before I'm crushed between the bridge and the rocky bottom.

Reaching up, he pushed beams apart until he saw light. Kalvin pulled and tore his way to the surface.

Finally, he broke free and rowed upstream to slow his speed. The bridge drifted away from him.

The stream is moving faster. Why is it picking up speed?

The banks had changed to rocky cliffs and the width of the stream had narrowed. Kalvin steered toward the middle of the stream to keep from being slammed into the rocks.

The bridge was jammed sideways between two large boulders. Kalvin was headed right for it. He rowed backwards as fast as he could, slowing his speed. His feet smashed into the bridge. The impact turned him sideways and the bridge began to move again.

Kalvin pushed away from the structure to keep from getting entangled again. Once more the bridge pulled away from him.

I'm still traveling too fast. The stream has narrowed some more.

The current pushed him toward the left cliff wall. He stretched out his left arms and pushed against the face of the cliff. Downstream part of the bridge shattered as it slammed into the rocks. A roar up ahead drew his attention. Kalvin watched as the front end of the bridge dropped down and the back end rose into the air. Then the back end dropped out of sight.

Oh, no, it's a waterfall! There's no way to prevent being swept over the falls.

CHAPTER FIVE

❧

LOST

The current banged Kalvin against a rock. He wrapped his upper right tentacle around the stone and held tight. His feet were at the edge of the waterfall. Water rushed over him. Debris from the swift water bounced off him.

If I can hold on long enough, the lake will drain away, Kalvin reasoned. *The water flow could be calm enough for me to walk out of this gorge.*

Kalvin thought he might succeed until a log mashed his tentacle against the rock. He lost his grip and he was swept over the falls. The waterfall wasn't very high, but the force of the water pushed him under. Kalvin was tossed about and dragged along the stream bottom. He popped to the surface and was slammed against the rocks. A jagged rock tore into his side. Kalvin cried out at the searing pain.

Kalvin tried pushing away from the rocky sides, but the strong current slammed him against the rocks again and again. Gradually, the stream began to calm. *I'm exhausted*, thought Kalvin. *I need to get to shore, but I feel so weak. My side hurts so much.* He became dizzy and then everything went black.

Kalvin didn't know how long he was unconscious. When he opened his eyes, all he saw was water. *I'm floating face down,* he realized. He pushed down with his left arm tentacles and rolled onto his back. The shore was hundreds of feet away and the water was very calm.

17

I'm in a lake, he thought. *My side still hurts very badly; I need to row to shore.*

His arms felt heavy as he paddled toward shore. Moving his right arms caused his side to hurt more.

Kalvin reached the shoreline. Holding onto a tree limb with his left arms, he slowly pulled himself up. He became dizzy and fell back into the lake. *I've got to get up*, he told himself. Weakness and a throbbing pain in his side would soon overcome him. He grabbed the limb again and pulled hard while his feet clawed into the shore. Kalvin slowly stood and clutched a tree to keep his balance. He gingerly felt the split in his side. A foot-long gash was between his upper and lower arms. Kalvin lifted the tentacle from his wound and stared at the tip of his arm. It was wet with green blood.

Maybe I won't bleed as badly, now that I'm out of the water, Kalvin hoped. *I don't know which way to go. This lake doesn't look familiar.* A few squirrels were gathering nuts nearby.

"Excuse me," Kalvin inquired. "Can any of you tell me where I am?"

"You're here," answered a squirrel.

"But where is here?" asked Kalvin. "What landmark is close to this lake?"

The squirrels gave him a blank stare.

"Are there any other kudzu monsters living near here?" asked Kalvin.

"Old Karrie lives near," answered a squirrel.

"She lives up the hill in the forest," said another.

"How will I find her?" Kalvin asked.

"Ask Charlie," a squirrel chimed in.

"Who or what is Charlie?" asked Kalvin.

"He's her fox. He comes to the lake every day."

Kalvin moved to the edge of the lake and fed for several hours. Feeding didn't ease his pain, but he felt stronger. While he wandered around the forest the rest of the day, he asked several small animals to tell Charlie or Karrie he was looking for them.

Kalvin rested and fed during the night. The next morning he awoke to find himself weaker than he was the day before. He touched his side; blood still leaked from the gash.

"I see why you're looking for me," said a fox at his feet. "You need to see Karrie before you bleed to death. Follow me and I'll take you to her."

Kalvin assumed the fox was Charlie and staggered after him. Charlie walked slowly and often stopped to wait on Kalvin.

"I think you should stop and rest for awhile," said Charlie. "I'll find Karrie and bring her to you."

"That sounds good to me," Kalvin replied. "Can she stop my bleeding?"

"She can save you," answered Charlie. "That's if I fetch her in time."

Kalvin watched the fox trot into the forest. He leaned against a tree and closed his eyes.

When he opened his eyes it was night again. He felt dizzy and something was being pressed against his wound. He reached down to feel the gash and a tentacle slapped his arm away.

"You leave that wound alone," said a stern female voice. Then everything faded into black again.

CHAPTER SIX

❦

KARRIE

Kalvin blinked a couple of times and opened his large black eyes. Nothing looked familiar. He began to remember what had happened and why he didn't recognize anything. His back was against a tree. He bowed up several of his feet and feeder roots began to break free.

I must have been resting here for several days, Kalvin reasoned. *Something is holding me against this tree.* Kalvin twisted to break free. Three pairs of arm tentacles unwrapped from around his body.

"So, you finally decided to wake up," said a raspy voice behind him. "Are you stable enough to stand by yourself, young monster?" repeated the voice.

"I, I feel okay," Kalvin stammered.

"Good, I've been holding you up for six days."

Six days, Kalvin reflected. *I can't believe I've been out for six days, but the trees are starting to lose their leaves. My kudzu leaves are turning brown.*

While Kalvin pondered his situation, a female kudzu monster moved into view. She was a little shorter than his mom and had two of her six arms folded. She had dark green oval-shaped eyes like all the females, but fewer kudzu vines.

Kalvin touched the wound on his side.

"My name is Karrie," said the female. "And you need to keep your tentacles off my poultice. You're healing nicely, considering how much blood you lost. Now you tell me your name, young monster."

"My name is Kalvin. I jumped in a stream after the dam broke and ended up unconscious in the lake."

"Why would you do a thing like that?" Karrie retorted.

"A young human girl fell in and was drowning. I saved her, but a bridge collapsed, drug me downstream, and I went over a waterfall."

"That sounds like quite an ordeal," replied Karrie. "Who are your parents?"

"My mother's name is Kitty and my father is Kleatus."

"I don't know Kitty, but I remember meeting a young monster named Kleatus about thirty years ago. So, you're his boy. I guess you are exploring on your own. Male kudzu monsters seem to do that when they're around twelve or thirteen years old."

"I'm eleven and a half," Kalvin replied. "I need to go home. I promised I would return home when my leaves started to turn."

"You need to take it easy while your gash is knitting together. You don't need to open that wound. Do you know how to get back home?"

"I'll go back to the lake and follow the stream back to where I fell in the water," answered Kalvin. "Also, I want to thank you for doctoring my wound and holding me for six days."

"You're welcome, Kalvin," smiled Karrie. "But there are three streams flowing into the lake. Do you know which one you came down?"

"I'm not sure. But the stream flowed from the northeast."

"Well that narrows it down to one of two streams. You hang around here for another week and try to figure out which stream to follow."

"Why don't you come with me?" asked Kalvin. "You could meet my mother and my sister, Kandi."

"Kalvin, I'm ninety years old," answered Karrie. "I don't take long trips anymore. You don't know where you're going and winter is a few weeks away. Charlie will take you back to the lake and show you the two streams."

Kalvin fed while he waited for Charlie to return. The fox arrived the next morning. Kalvin felt stronger each day. His side itched, so Karrie changed his poultice before she let him follow Charlie.

22

"Don't bother that poultice; it'll fall off in four or five days," Karrie instructed him. "I want you to listen to Charlie and do like he tells you."

"I will," promised Kalvin. "Thank you again for all you've done for me. Is there anything I can do for you?"

"Yes, there is something you can do," answered Karrie. "I'll need your help this spring with the creepers. You can bring your family with you to help."

"What are creepers?"

"They're bad critters. Your father knows about them. He helped me with them once before."

Kalvin turned and followed after Charlie. Charlie didn't speak as he led the way to the lake, unlike Squiggy, who chattered constantly when he rode on Kalvin's shoulder. They arrived at the lake within the hour.

"Karrie told me you had to rest for fifteen minutes every hour," Charlie told him. "I can take you to the first stream today. Tomorrow we'll go to the other stream."

"I need to start home," answered Kalvin. "When winter comes the ground will freeze at night and make it hard for me to walk."

"Karrie told me you would argue, but you have to take it easy until you heal."

The next day Kalvin saw the other stream. Neither looked familiar.

"I'm going to follow this stream," Kalvin told Charlie. "Thank you for your help."

"You're welcome, Kalvin; I enjoyed your company and learning about your family and your friend, Squiggy. I've never heard of a kudzu monster having a human friend like your sister Kandi had. Take care, Kalvin; don't reopen that wound."

"I'll be careful," Kalvin hollered after Charlie as the fox disappeared into the woods.

I should wait until tomorrow before I set out on another journey, thought Kalvin. *But I need to get home before Dad and Mom start to worry. I can travel for several hours before dark and then I'll rest. A few more days and I'll be able to travel day and night.*

Kalvin continued to follow the stream and stopped every couple of hours until his poultice began to fall off. Kalvin felt a rough scar on his side, but it didn't hurt anymore. Most of the trees were bare and his leaves were brown and started falling as he moved. The nights were cold, and he didn't walk while frost was on the ground.

It wouldn't do for me to fall on frozen ground, thought Kalvin. *I haven't fallen on ice in years, but a fall could open that wound.* He had been walking for a week when the stream became wider and emptied into a river.

Oh, great, I've been following the wrong stream.

A large bridge was down the river and hundreds of cars crossed it every minute. When the sun had set, he noticed a bright light glowing further down the river. He began to follow the river toward the light.

What could cause that much light? He needed to climb a hill and investigate that glow.

Kalvin pushed with his feet and pulled on trees as he climbed the hill. The lights grew brighter the closer he got to the top. When he crested the hill, he couldn't believe his eyes.

CHAPTER SEVEN

❦

THE BIG CITY

A great city stretched before his eyes. *I've never seen so many lights,* thought Kalvin. *Cars are everywhere and the roads have more lanes. The buildings are taller than the biggest trees, and hundreds of people are walking along the sidewalks. Even the trees along the sidewalks have small white lights draped around their bare branches.*

In the store windows were small evergreen trees decorated with red and green lights. Colored glass balls and other decorations hung from their limbs. Many of the people carried packages and shopping bags.

It must be getting close to that winter holiday I've seen in other towns, but I've never seen so much activity. Kandi tried explaining what that holiday was about, but I wasn't listening. She learned about it from her human friend, Maranda. I should have listened to her more carefully.

These people are in such a hurry and they honk their car horns more than in the small towns. They don't seem as friendly.

Kalvin moved down the hill toward the city. *It's easier to move through the brush with my leaves gone,* thought Kalvin. But then a kudzu vine became caught on a tree limb and broke off. *That won't grow back until the spring.*

Kalvin walked behind a levee with train tracks running along the top. He could see a road on the other side of the bank. *I'll go to my left. The buildings are lower and there are less people. I should head back, but*

I want to explore the city. I'll wait a few more hours and see if the traffic dies down. Then, I'll cross the road.

Kalvin waited a couple of hours, but the cars continued to flow down the road.

I'll go in the other direction as far as I can.

As he approached the spot where he came up from the forest, he noticed most of the people were gone. Many of the stores had turned off their lights. A stray dog trotted across the tracks and headed down to the road. The stray crossed the road and began sniffing along the sidewalk.

In the distance a dark shape moved slowly along the tracks toward Kalvin. *It doesn't look like a dog,* thought Kalvin as he moved toward the shape. It looked like an injured man. The man staggered and fell on the tracks. Kalvin heard a train whistle and pushed toward the man as fast as he could. *I don't see a train headlight, but the tracks curve into a tunnel. I need to reach the injured man before a train pops out of that tunnel!*

The man was unconscious and sprawled across the tracks. Kalvin was only a few yards away when a light shone out of the tunnel. He pushed up the levee as the train raced out of the tunnel. *It's really coming fast and I can't make much speed up this steep levee!*

All of a sudden a bright light shone in Kalvin's eyes. The train was less than a hundred feet away. Kalvin stretched out an arm tentacle and grabbed the man's leg. Kalvin drug him off the tracks as the train rumbled past.

I hope I didn't injure him more by dragging him, but the train would have killed him.

The man began to moan and pulled a bottle out of his coat pocket.

That bottle may have the man's medicine in it.

The man sat up, unscrewed the cap off the bottle and began to pour liquid into his mouth, some of which ran down his chin.

He seems to be feeling better; he's getting to his feet and singing.

The man stood up, lost his balance, rolled down the hill and broke his bottle. *I need to find help for him. I'll carry him to the edge of the road. Someone in a car will see him and take him to the doctor.*

Kalvin carried the unconscious man to the edge of the road and sat him down in the grass. He stood close to the man in case he woke up and tried to stagger onto the street. Several cars passed by, but no one stopped. Finally one car stopped, but the man remained in the car.

I wonder why he doesn't get out and help the poor man. Maybe he's waiting for help to move him.

A few minutes later a car arrived with blue lights flashing. A policeman exited the car and walked over to the man. The officer shook the man until he woke up.

"Do you have any identification?" asked the policeman.

The man climbed to his feet and tried to run away before the police officer grabbed his arm.

"Okay, we're going to the station," said the officer.

He helped the man into the back seat of the police car and drove away.

I knew the policeman would help him, Kalvin thought. *They're always helping people. Oh, there's that dog in an alley trying to get into a metal container. Maybe there's food in that can and the dog can't get to it.*

The dog ran deeper into the alley as Kalvin crossed the road and dumped everything from the can onto the sidewalk.

Another good deed, thought Kalvin, as the dog rushed from the shadows and began digging through the garbage.

I better head back. It'll be dawn in a few hours and more people will be out.

There were houses along the street instead of tall buildings. They were all dark and no one was about except for one house. A man stood out in the yard by an opened window. Another man in the house was handing things to him through the window. The man at the window took the items to a brown van and went back for more. Both men were dressed in black and moved very quietly. They loaded several more things in the van before the man in the house crawled out the window. They didn't shut the window and drove away without turning on their van lights.

I think those men were taking things that didn't belong to them, Kalvin reasoned. Kalvin followed in the direction the van had gone.

CHAPTER EIGHT

❧

THE THIEVES

Kalvin knew he should head back to the stream and follow it to the lake, but he wanted to see if he could find the thieves.

I won't have much help locating that brown van with the dent. Most of the small animals are asleep during the winter. I'll look around for a couple of days before I head back downstream.

Kalvin explored the city some more as he searched for the van. Near the end of the second day he came to another highway. It was late at night, but dozens of cars and trucks drove past every minute.

I can't go any further this way, thought Kalvin. *I need to turn around and head back the way I came.*

Kalvin rested during the day and traveled all night. The next morning he stopped close to where two roads intersected. While resting he saw a brown van approaching. The van had the big dent and it turned on the side road.

I'll travel down that road. If I don't spot the van, I'll head back to the lake. I've wasted two days trying to find that van. Maybe chasing them is just an excuse to keep exploring new territory. My family is probably worried sick about me. I should be headed home.

Kalvin debated what to do. He decided to continue looking for one more night and head home if he didn't find the van.

There weren't many houses on this road and very few cars. He searched all night and didn't find the van. Kalvin spotted a field covered in kudzu vines.

That'll be a good place to spend the day. Ill blend in with the other vine-covered trees.

In the middle of the field was a small abandoned house. The house was covered with vines and had started to rot.

Something is not right about that house, thought Kalvin. *Some of the boards in the roof look new and the back door doesn't have any vines on it. The vines are cut away and there is a new padlock on the door. There's a faint path that leads from the door to the road. Nobody would live here. The windows are covered with boards, but there are cracks between them I can look through.*

Kalvin peered through a crack. The house was dark, but it seemed to have a lot of stuff stacked inside.

I want to see who is using this abandoned house for storage. I'll stay another night and see if anyone comes here.

Early the next morning a police car drove past. Kalvin watched all day, but no one came to the house. Near dusk the same police car drove past going the other way. Kalvin knew it was the same car because it had the same number painted on the car. Kalvin watched that night, but nobody showed up.

The sun rose and Kalvin watched the police car drive past.

He must live close by, thought Kalvin. *I'll stay until night before heading back.*

Kalvin watched the house a second day. Only two cars and three trucks drove past during the day. One of the cars was the police officer returning home. The sun set and Kalvin decided to hang around for a few more hours. Midnight passed and dawn was only a few hours away when the brown van stopped on the road. The van didn't have any lights on and two men exited the truck. Before opening the back of the van, they looked around and then carried some electronic goods toward the shack. One of them pulled a key from his pocket, unlocked the padlock and carried the stuff into the building.

That's the men who robbed that house and this is where they keep the stolen goods, Kalvin concluded.

When they emptied the van, they carried a television set and some other loot from the building to the van. The thieves locked the door, started the van and drove away without turning on the headlights. A short distance away the brake lights came on.

The men turned to the left, I'll walk up there and see what road they took.

When Kalvin got to where the van had turned, he found a dirt road. After a couple of hundred feet the dirt road ended at an old house.

This isn't a road. It's a long driveway.

The van was parked behind the house. Kalvin slid close to the house. A light was on and Kalvin heard the men talking.

"We can doze for awhile, said one of the men. Jake will be here at sunrise to buy the stuff loaded in the van. He'll be back tomorrow to buy the rest."

"I'm glad to be rid of those stolen goods," said the other one.

I need to find a way to capture the thieves and return the stolen items. There are very few cars or people around. That's why the men feel safe hiding their stolen goods so close to where they live. That police car will drive by in the morning. If Jake is coming at sunrise, he should be here before the police officer drives by. Maybe I can alert the officer.

Kalvin came up with a plan, but he had to hurry; the sun would be up in an hour.

CHAPTER NINE

❧

COPS AND ROBBERS

I need to find something to jam under the van, thought Kalvin, *to keep them from leaving.*

He looked around for some large item around the yard and spotted a tree stump in the front yard. The light in the house had gone out.

The men must be asleep; I'll have to be careful not to make a lot of noise.

Kalvin wrapped his lower arm tentacles around the stump and pulled as hard as he could. The stump loosened a little, but the tree roots still held tight. Kalvin tried rocking the stump from side to side. The stump's roots were anchored too deeply in the earth. The stump barely moved.

I need to find something else. It will take too much time for me to pull up the stump. The brick steps at the back of the house aren't attached to anything. They shouldn't weigh more than five or six hundred pounds.

Kalvin reached down with his lower arms and pulled the steps away from the house. Picking them up was harder than he thought.

I think these steps are closer to seven hundred pounds. I'll pick up the back of the van with my upper arms and toss the steps under the rear wheels.

Kalvin had to set the steps down twice before he reached the van. He tried but couldn't lift the van while he held the steps. *This isn't working. I'll set the steps down, pick up the rear of the van and slide the steps under with my lower arms.*

Kalvin lifted the van, but couldn't slide the steps over the rough ground. He lifted the back end of the van and drug the vehicle over the steps. When he eased the van down, the back wheels were a foot off the ground. Kalvin tugged on the license plate. The tearing metal made a loud creaking sound. Kalvin paused for a minute and watched the house, but luckily no lights came on.

I have to be careful not to make that much noise again. I'll bend the tag back and forth until it breaks loose.

It took Kalvin longer than he liked, but he broke the tag free. Clutching the tag in one arm, he started toward the end of the driveway. On the way he picked up three large rocks. The first rays of sunshine shone in the eastern sky. Kalvin stopped at the edge of the road and watched a truck pass by. A little later a U-haul truck turned up the driveway.

When the U-haul disappeared up the driveway, Kalvin set the rocks down at the front of the driveway.

They're not as big as I wanted, but it'll take them a few minutes to remove them. I need to get to the shack before the police car comes this way.

Kalvin pulled and pushed himself through the kudzu patch to the abandoned house. He tore the back door off its hinges, entered the shack and took a computer.

I've got to hurry; time is running out, he thought as he placed the computer in the brush near the side of the road. He returned to the shack and carried out a TV and a small chest full of jewelry.

I'll place the TV beside the house where it can be seen from the road. Kalvin placed the van tag on the television and the jewelry box on top of the tag.

That will do nicely, he said to himself. *Now I need a way to stop the police car. I hope it is the next vehicle to drive by. I can't toss any of the stolen goods on the road; it would destroy them. I need something small that won't cause him to wreck.*

Kalvin picked up a small stick about two feet long. As he moved toward the road, he picked up a second stick that was a little bigger but was more rotted than the first.

I'll throw both of them, he decided. *They won't damage the car and two sticks hitting in the road in front of him should make him stop. What if he doesn't stop? If he doesn't stop, my plan won't work. Maybe I better toss them so they'll hit the car. But if I get closer to the road to hit the car, he might see me throw them.*

Kalvin picked up two more sticks and spotted a vehicle coming down the road. Kalvin held a stick in each of his four arm tentacles. A car rounded the curve and began to slow down. A woman in the car had spotted the computer.

I can't let her take the computer, thought Kalvin. *But what can I do without revealing myself?*

Suddenly, the police car rounded the curve. The woman stepped on the gas pedal and drove away. As the police car reached the kudzu patch, four sticks sailed in front of it. The first hit the road in front of the car. The rest hit the car hood, the front windshield and the top of the car. Smoke came from the tires as the police officer hit the brakes. Kalvin froze in place.

A red-faced policeman exited the car and stood looking around the field. He looked straight at Kalvin.

"Whoever threw those sticks is in a lot of trouble," yelled the police officer. "You had better come out of hiding. If I have to catch you, you'll be in more trouble."

The policeman waited a little while, talked on his police radio to headquarters and then moved toward the house. Suddenly, the officer stopped and looked behind Kalvin. He bent down and picked up something. Kalvin heard him walking toward the shack. A few minutes later he walked past Kalvin with the jewelry box and tag in his hand.

The policeman began talking into his police radio.

"This is car 122," he said. "I found what appears to be a stash of stolen goods in an abandoned house off the Old Stanton Road. I'll need backup and a trace on license tag THF-3694."

Kalvin closed one eye on the side where the officer stood and watched with his other eye. Several minutes later the U-haul stopped in front of the rocks in the driveway. A small man jumped out of the U-haul and tried to move one of the stones. He succeeded in pushing it to the side of the driveway when two more police cars and a police van arrived. The man climbed into the U-haul and watched as the policemen started to carry the loot to the police van.

The man in the U-haul panicked and plowed over the other two rocks and spun onto the road. As he raced away a small stream of oil poured from his cracked oil pan. Blue lights flashed on a police car and its tires squealed as the car rocketed after the U-haul.

Kalvin heard the police station call back and tell the officer that the tag belonged to a man who lived just down the street. More police cars arrived and several policemen walked up the driveway and moved through the woods toward the house.

I can't hear what's happening at the house, but the police will find stolen goods in the locked van and probably more in the house. The police have probably caught the U-haul. There's nothing more I can do, but I'll wait and see what happens.

It was mid-morning before the stolen goods were removed. Kalvin saw a police car drive by with the two crooks in the back seat.

During the day Kalvin thought of his family. *I should have been home three weeks ago. I'll follow the stream back to the lake, then follow the other stream back up to where I jumped in the water. But it'll be weeks before I'm home again.*

CHAPTER TEN

༄

WINTER STORM

Kalvin followed the stream toward the lake. The weather was much colder. Ice formed during the night and Kalvin was forced to walk slower on the slippery ground. All of his kudzu leaves had turned brown and had fallen to the ground. Kalvin looked like a very spooky tree. He traveled most of the days and all the nights for a week until he reached the lake. Twice there was a light snow that made the ground more slippery and forced him to travel very slowly.

It's mid-afternoon, thought Kalvin. *I've been walking for four days and nights without rest. I'll stay here and feed, then follow the other stream tonight.*

Even though it was the warm part of the day, it was difficult for his feeder roots to burrow into the frozen ground. Around midnight he pulled his feeder roots free and followed the edge of the lake until he found the other stream leading north. Kalvin followed the stream for three days and nights before he spotted the little community where the girl had fallen in the water.

Well, the day is dawning and I'm on the side of the stream where the houses are located. I better cross the stream to the other side.

He held onto trees going down the bank. Picking a spot where tree limbs stretched across the stream, Kalvin waded into the waist-deep water, held onto the limbs above him and pushed across very slowly.

He inched up the other bank by pulling on trees and clawing at the ground with his feet tentacles. After traveling slowly over several hills, he found a familiar path.

This is better, thought Kalvin. *I'll rest until night. If I travel day and night, I should be home in five or six days.* As he rested, snowflakes began to fall. Several minutes later the snow was falling harder.

Oh, great, my poor feet had enough trouble pushing and pulling across this hard ground. Now I'll have to travel with an inch or two of snow on the ground!

Kalvin rested and fed until nightfall. It had snowed all day. Instead of an inch or two of snow, which is normal for this part of the country, six to eight inches were on the ground. Early that night Kalvin started his journey home. He couldn't see the ground, but no trees grew where the path had been. As Kalvin pushed through the snow, he plowed a deep rut behind him.

That's going to be confusing to any human that crosses my path, thought Kalvin, *a trench in the snow that leads to a tree.*

He continued to travel along the path until it forked. Kalvin wasn't sure which path to take. When he had traveled through here two months ago, he had moved through the woods and avoided the path. He had been traveling northwest. One path branched to the north and the other to the east. Kalvin decided to follow the northern path.

Everything looks different with all the leaves gone from the trees and bushes and the snow on the ground. No animals are around to help me. They're sleeping or staying in their burrows because of the deep snow.

Kalvin followed the path, which turned east and later southeast. He hoped it would change direction, but later that night he came to a dry lake bed. His heart sank as he realized this was the lake where the dam had broken. He had gone in a circle.

Ahead he saw the little community where he had saved the girl. *I'll go back to the houses and retrace my steps from there. It's late at night and they'll still be asleep.*

Kalvin traveled to the little neighborhood and saw that two of the houses had been washed away and most of the people had lost their decks. The bridge was gone, but he was on the right side of the stream. He followed the road a short distance until he came to a tree that had fallen across the road.

I'm tired; I'll rest beside the road, he thought, as he closed his large round eyes.

Kalvin had been pushing himself hard to get home and he hadn't rested enough. He fell into a deep sleep and dreamed that he was standing by a lake and the tree leaves were green. The little forest animals were playing with his sister, Kandi. He could hear the roar of a waterfall emptying into the lake. The sound of the waterfall grew louder and louder. Suddenly he awoke to the sound of a chainsaw. Someone was cutting wood behind him.

Oh, no, It's morning! The people are up. Someone is cutting firewood and I might be next!

The chainsaw went silent and Kalvin heard the crunching sound of someone walking through the snow.

"Do you want some help clearing the road?" a man's voice asked.

"Sure," said the man with the chainsaw. "With your help we'll have this tree off the road in under an hour."

Whew, thought Kalvin, *they're just removing the dead tree from the road.*

The chainsaw started cutting again and a short time later, branches began falling down the hill close to Kalvin.

The other man must be throwing the limbs down here as they're cut from the dead tree.

Suddenly, Kalvin felt a jolt that almost knocked him over. A log from the tree had rolled down the hill and slammed into him. A minute later another log rolled past him. Kalvin braced his feet and slowly stretched an arm to push against another tree. He had just touched the tree when a thicker log than the first one bounced into him.

It's a good thing I was pushing against the tree, thought Kalvin, *that log would have knocked me over.*

Two more logs grazed him before the men finished clearing the road. When they walked away, Kalvin resumed his journey home. He had to move slowly because it was colder than the day before and the snow was frozen into ice. The next day was much warmer and the ice was melting fast. Kalvin still had to move slowly, because the melting ice made the ground slippery.

He stopped at night and rested until noon the next day. The only small animal Kalvin saw was a raccoon trudging through a patch of snow on a distant hill. There were no animals to warn him of approaching danger. A hundred feet in front of him a flock of birds took flight. Kalvin sensed danger.

Something frightened those birds. I'll hold perfectly still and see what scared them.

CHAPTER ELEVEN

∾

MISSING

Kalvin watched as something pushed through the bushes in his direction. He couldn't tell what it was. It crept very slowly and stayed hidden in the bushes. The thing stopped behind a large oak tree. Kalvin didn't move and waited to see what it would do. What looked like a walking tree stump slid from behind the oak. It had light green oval-shaped eyes. It was his little sister!

"Kandi?" Kalvin exclaimed.

"Kalvin!" Kandi shouted. She rushed forward with outstretched tentacles and hugged him. Kalvin hugged her back.

"What are you doing out here alone?" he asked.

"Mom's down the hill. We were looking for you and Dad."

"What! Dad's missing?"

"Dad left last week to see if our friends Karl and Karen had seen you. He should have returned in a few days, but he didn't. Mom started worrying and decided we'd go look for both of you."

"Kalvin, I was so worried about you," said a voice behind him.

Kalvin turned and saw his mother pushing up the hill.

"Mom!" Kalvin yelled. He pushed toward her as fast as he could go. Kitty hugged Kalvin as Kandi rushed over to hug them both.

"Well, you're with us again," said Kitty, "and your father is missing."

"I guess we should head toward Karl and Karen's place," added Kalvin.

"Kandi, you look skinny without your leaves," laughed Kalvin.

"I look the same as I did last winter," replied Kandi. "Except I'm nearly four and a half feet tall and that's a foot taller than last year."

"You'll grow much slower in the coming years," replied Kitty.

"I don't remember your having that big scar on your side last year, Kalvin," said Kandi.

"Scar!" shouted Kitty as she turned Kalvin to look at his side.

Kalvin told them all the things that had happened to him since he left home.

"That explains why you didn't return home before winter," said Kitty.

They had only been pushing toward Karl and Karen's for a couple of hours when Kitty spotted Karen headed their way.

"Karen," hollered Kitty. "Have you seen Kleatus?"

"Yes," she shouted back. "He arrived at our place yesterday."

"Yesterday?" Kitty questioned. "He should have gotten to your place days ago."

"Kleatus said he had to leave the trail because of the deer hunters camped along it. That was the night it snowed. He was crossing what he thought was a field but it was a frozen lake. The ice broke and he plunged waist deep into the water. Kleatus had to break the ice as he slowly walked. Before he could climb out people arrived and cut holes in the ice to fish. Kleatus couldn't move, and the lake froze around him even thicker than before. He had to remain there until the sun warmed the ice enough for him to break free.

When he reached the edge of the lake he slipped on the mud and fell on his face. There weren't any trees around the lake big enough for him to pull to his feet. He had to crawl across a field to some large trees. Kleatus said he slipped half a dozen times trying to pull up.

While he was with us, a raccoon arrived and said he heard a young kudzu monster had been badly hurt and was with Karrie. Karl and Kleatus left to see Karrie, and I started toward your place to report what happened."

Karen finished her tale and looked at Kalvin. "I see Kalvin is with you. He looks fine to me."

"Karrie patched him up," answered Kitty.

"I think we should go to Karrie's, too," added Kalvin. "She will need our help in the spring to fight the creepers."

"Oh, dear," moaned Karen, "the creepers are on the move again."

"What are creepers?" whispered Kandi.

"They are nasty creatures that eat everything in their path," answered Kitty. "Kleatus fought those things years ago before we even met. He said they were shaggy and grayish green with yellow teeth and eyes. Their bodies are two to four feet long with eight to twelve tentacles that stretch ten to fifteen feet in length. They kind of look like huge long-legged spiders covered with moss.

"Karl and I were with Kleatus when he fought them," Karen added. "There were around two hundred of the creatures. The creeper queen was with them. She was huge and she had slanted red eyes and big yellow teeth coated with a green mold. She disappeared into a large lake and stayed underwater. We never saw her again. Karrie said she'd stay down there and eat fish for weeks before she snuck back to the swamps."

CHAPTER TWELVE

∾

THE REUNION

After several days of traveling through the forest, they neared Karrie's dwelling. Kalvin saw his dad and Karl coming to meet them.

"Charlie the fox told us you were headed this way," said Kleatus. "Karrie told us how you had been injured and healed. She said you went to the big city. I'd like you to take me there sometime."

"Sure, Dad," Kalvin responded. "That would be great!"

"No one is going anywhere until we've talked this over among ourselves," Kitty insisted. "We're staying here and resting for a few days."

Everyone hugged and greeted Karrie. Kalvin and Kleatus retold mishaps and adventures to everyone. They decided to spend the rest of the winter with Karrie. A couple of weeks passed before Kitty agreed that Kalvin and Kleatus could travel to the city. Karl had seen the city and wasn't interested in going with them.

"I want to go with Dad and Kalvin to the city," Kandi pleaded with her mom.

"No, you stay with me," answered Kitty. "Karrie has much she wants to teach us while we're here."

"We'll only be gone a few weeks." Kalvin tried to ease Kandi's disappointment.

"That's what you said the last time," Kitty replied. "Be back before three weeks or else I'll come looking for you this time."

"We'll be back before three weeks are up; I promise."

"We need to make our plan for fighting the creepers in the spring," added Karrie.

Kalvin and Kleatus set out for the city. The cold weather wasn't as bad now, but the morning frost made the ground slippery most mornings. It was around the first of March, so spring was near.

On the sixth day of their trip, they spotted the lights of the city.

"We'd better stay on the fringes of the city, Dad. It's crowded with people."

"That sounds like a smart plan to me, Son. We don't want to be observed walking around."

"There's a stream in the forest that borders the city for miles. We can follow it during the day. Late at night we can creep up to the railroad tracks and get a better look at the city."

Around two o'clock in the morning they pushed up to the railroad tracks.

"Wow, Kalvin, those buildings are as high as you said they were. I can't believe so many cars are driving around this late."

"People are out and about at all hours in the city, Dad."

They stayed there for a couple of hours and then moved back to the stream. Dawn was just breaking when they came to a large highway bridge. Hundreds of cars and trucks were crossing the bridge into the city every minute.

"There are more people and cars than I ever imagined."

"It's a big city, Dad. We'd better wait here the rest of the day and evening until midnight. Then we can cross under the bridge and go to a wooded area close to the city where the tallest buildings are located."

Late that night they crossed under the bridge and traveled about a mile until they came to the small grove of trees that overlooked the main part of the city.

"These building have sixty to seventy floors to them, Dad."

"Yes, I can see them. There must be people working in the buildings, because a lot of the lights are still on."

"A few of the lights are left on all the time, and people live in some of the buildings."

They stayed motionless in the grove all day. Thousands of people hustled along on the busy streets and sidewalks. People sat on the benches close to them. Some even ate their lunch there. One man walked his dog through the grove and the dog wet on Kleatus' foot. It was all Kalvin could do not to laugh out loud.

Late the next night they left the grove of trees and followed the stream back under the bridge.

"I've seen the city and it was impressive, but we'd better head back to Karrie's."

They were following the stream on the outskirts of the city. A road was at the top of a levy next to the stream, which was getting wider as they followed it out of town. Dawn was just breaking when they were startled by a loud bang.

"Someone is shooting a gun!" exclaimed Kleatus, as he looked about.

"It came from the road above the stream, Dad."

Just then, a small car veered off the road in front of a bridge that crossed the stream. The vehicle flipped over and rolled down the hill. It came to a halt upside down in the stream.

"The driver may be hurt, Dad, and water is pouring into the car. We need to save him before he drowns."

CHAPTER THIRTEEN

❧

THE RESCUE

Kalvin and Kleatus pushed through the water to the car.

"Kalvin, go to the back of the car and I'll take the front. Let's try to turn the car over and put it right side up."

Kalvin held onto the rocky bottom with his feet tentacles and grabbed the back bumper with his arm tentacles.

"When I count to three, try to flip the car. One, two, three," shouted Kleatus.

They pulled the car onto its side. The driver was out of the water and hanging unconscious from his seat belt.

"Let's push the car back onto its tires," said Kleatus.

"One of the front tires has a large hole in it, Dad. I guess that's what caused the car to veer off the road."

They pushed on the car and it toppled over right side up.

"Dad, two cars drove by while we were flipping the car over and they didn't stop. The car might not be spotted for hours. Do you think we can pull it up the bank close to the road?"

"We could try. It's a small car. I'll take the front end, because the motor makes it heavier than the back. Let's pick it up and turn the car around. I want to go up the bank first. If I see any cars coming, we can put the car down and pretend we're trees." Kalvin strained as he picked up the rear of the car a few feet off the stream bottom. The car was still

49

in about a foot of water as he pushed slowly toward the bank. It looked like his father struggled with his load as well. As the car came out of the water, it seemed to gain weight. Kalvin lifted the car a little higher so he could use his upper arms as well.

"Put the car down, Kalvin; a car is coming."

Kalvin eased the car to the ground and held still. He noticed a lot of water running out of the car. The other car drove past them and over the bridge.

"Okay, pick the car back up. If we carry it a few more yards, I think it will be seen," said Kleatus.

Although a lot of water had run out of the car, it didn't seem much lighter to Kalvin. They had only carried it a few more yards when Kalvin spotted a motorcycle coming the other way.

"Put the car down, Dad; a motorcycle is coming behind you."

The motorcycle crossed the bridge on the other side of the road and kept going. Kalvin spotted a truck coming toward them. *A truck driver sits higher*, thought Kalvin. *Maybe the truck driver will see the wrecked car.*

The truck drove past them then stopped on the bridge and backed up.

A man stepped out of the truck. He ran up to the car and tried to open the door, but it was locked. He ran up to the road and flagged down the next car he saw. A woman was in the other car, but she didn't get out.

"Do you have a cell phone?" yelled the man.

"Yes, I have a phone," she answered.

"Good, call 911. A man is injured in a car down the embankment."

A few minutes later the police arrived and forced the door open. Kalvin and Kleatus watched in silence as an ambulance arrived and the unconscious man was carried away on a stretcher.

"He'll be okay," said one of the men as he carried the stretcher to the ambulance. "But I have no idea why he and the inside of the car are soaked with water."

"I noticed that," said the policeman. "The ground is wet behind the car like someone lifted the car out of that stream and carried it up the bank."

"Superman must have flown by and spotted the wreck," said the man from the truck.

Everyone laughed, but the policeman was scratching his head and looking about.

"Someone with a wrecker must have pulled him out," said the police officer. "But why didn't he pull the car up to the road, and why did he leave?"

Kalvin and his dad waited until a wrecker removed the car and everyone had driven away before they started their journey.

"We need to hurry toward Karrie's," said Kleatus. "Spring must be near, because our kudzu leaves have started to bud."

The weather was warmer and the ground wasn't frozen in the morning, so they made very good time going back. When they arrived at Karrie's they were covered with kudzu leaves.

Karrie called them together and told them about the creepers.

"You know a lot more about the creepers now," she said. "They will probably be passing through here in a few weeks, but I want to start patrolling the forest tomorrow. The little animals are coming out of hibernation and need to be told about the danger. We're going to split up and each monster will patrol a certain part of the forest. You will each have a squirrel or a fox with you. If you see a creeper, don't attack it. Send word to the others of their location by the squirrel or fox. Creepers are good at hiding and will try to ambush you if they can. They usually travel at night, but don't count on it"

"Kandi is remaining with me," said Kitty. Everyone agreed that was a good idea.

Kalvin and a squirrel named Smitty patrolled his section every night for three weeks with no sign of a creeper. Kleatus was half a mile away on his right and his mother and Kandi half a mile away on his left.

Late one evening Kalvin was watching a thicket when he noticed that rabbits and mice were leaving the field. Kalvin stopped a rabbit family.

"Why is everyone leaving the field?" he asked.

"Something evil is in the field and is eating little animals," answered the daddy rabbit.

Suddenly, Kalvin noticed something large moving in the thicket. He spotted three creepers, each about two feet long with eight legs about as big around as a garden hose. They looked like they were covered with moss and small leaves grew on their legs.

"Smitty," Kalvin said to the squirrel. "Go tell my dad there are creepers in my area."

Smitty ran off to his left.

"Smitty, you're going the wrong way," said Kalvin as he pointed to the right.

The squirrel changed direction and raced into the forest barking warnings as he ran.

When Kalvin turned toward the thicket, he saw three pairs of round yellow eyes watching him. The creepers turned and started moving slowly away from him. Kalvin gripped the club he had made and began to follow the creepers to keep them in his sight.

The creepers look like they could move fast with those long legs, thought Kalvin, *but they move their legs in slow motion. I guess that's why they're called creepers.*

After a couple of minutes he heard something running through the thicket toward him. It was Smitty.

"Kalvin," he squealed. "I didn't make it to your dad. There are more creepers behind us."

Kalvin turned and saw five creepers emerge from the forest. These were bigger than the three he was following. They were three to four feet long with more legs. They were coming down the hill toward him, and the three he was following had turned toward him, too. Smitty ran up Kalvin and sat on his upper left shoulder.

Oh, no! They've lured me into a trap. I'm caught between the two groups with no help on the way.

CHAPTER FOURTEEN

⤳

THE CREEPERS

There's too many of them for me to fight. I need to make a run for it and find help.

Kalvin looked around for an escape route and decided to run east. He stretched feet tentacles as far as he could to get more speed. As he hurried he gave a loud holler of alarm, his voice echoing through the forest. He glanced to his left and saw the five bigger creepers had moved quickly down the hill and were entering the thicket. The three smaller ones were close behind him. The larger creepers seemed to be moving through the thicket a little slower than he was, but he could hear the smaller ones staying close to him.

"The three creepers are gaining on us," Smitty chattered. "You're flattening the field as you plow through the thicket and it makes an easy path for the creepers to follow."

"We're pulling away from the larger ones though," answered Kalvin.

It seems the smaller creepers move faster. I should have made more than one club. An extra club would make a big difference if I have to make a stand and fight the creepers.

Kalvin reached the edge of the thicket and pushed into the forest. He let out another warning shout, which started the squirrels chattering around the forest.

Good, the squirrels are taking up the alarm. What! Something just grabbed my leg.

It felt like a thick cable wrapped around one of his foot tentacles.

"A creeper is holding onto your leg," squealed Smitty, "and you're dragging him behind you."

"Are the other two close enough to grab me, Smitty?"

"No, but they will be in a minute."

Teeth bit into the entangled foot tentacle. Kalvin passed the club to his lower right arm tentacle and began to beat behind him where the creeper had bitten him. The club broke in half, but the biting stopped and his foot was free.

"You clobbered him good," barked Smitty. "He's wiggling on the ground."

Kalvin came to a clearing in the woods and ran toward a small tree. He wrapped his two lower arm tentacles around it and began to pull.

If I can pull this out of the ground it will make a good weapon.

He turned around as he pulled at the tree. The other two creepers were nearly to him. Kalvin felt the tree tearing loose from the ground as he desperately tugged on the trunk. The two creepers bared their wedged-shaped yellow teeth as they charged at him. The tree broke free of the ground, and Kalvin swung the root ball at the closest creeper. The creeper sprang backwards, grabbed onto the tree and was jerked into the air. Kalvin slammed him into the ground, but the creature continued to hold onto the tree. Smitty jumped up and down on Kalvin's shoulder and chattered loudly at the creepers. Kalvin swung the tree in the opposite direction with the small creeper still holding on. He aimed the tree at the other creeper and let go. The tree and both creepers crashed into a pile as the other five creepers moved into the clearing. Kalvin turned and hurried toward the forest with five creepers close behind him.

"The two small ones look shaky, but they're up and headed our way," Smitty squeaked in Kalvin's ear slot.

Kalvin hoped he was headed toward his father, but he wasn't sure. Kudzu vines were being torn from his arms and body as he fled through the forest.

"How close are the creepers?" shouted Kalvin. "I don't hear any noise behind me."

"They're about ten yards behind you," barked Smitty. "They don't make much noise when they move through the forest."

Kalvin caught sight of two large creepers on his right side.

"Smitty, how did those two creepers get over on my right side?"

"They're two new ones and you still have seven behind you."

I guess my shouts must have alerted those other creepers.

Kalvin spotted a large stick on the ground that would make a good club, but he'd have to stop to pick it up. He made a decision and stopped for the club. As he picked it up, a tentacle wrapped around his lower left arm. Kalvin swung the club and knocked the creeper away just as it opened its mouth to bite him. The others were too close for him to run so he backed up to a large oak tree and raised his club.

All the creepers stopped and seemed to be deciding how to attack this armed monster. They split into groups. Four creepers faced him, two moved to his left and the other three moved to his right side. Although his earlier shout had alerted more creepers, Kalvin let out a loud bellow that roared through the forest. A deeper shout came from his right. Kalvin recognized his father's answering war cry.

When the creepers heard his father's shout they made hissing sounds and charged Kalvin on three sides. Kalvin slammed his club on a large one to his right and black blood splashed out of it. One creeper was dead, but dozens of tentacles were wrapping around his lower arms and body. Kalvin transferred the club to his upper right arm and smashed a three-foot creeper that bit his lower left arm.

That's two of them dead, but my arm is bleeding where it bit me.

Another creeper was about to bite one of his feet tentacles when a large rock sailed out of the woods and crushed him. Kalvin saw his father throw a second rock with such force that it sank into a creeper and icky black blood rushed out of its body. The last five broke off the attack and scattered into the forest, but not until the slowest one got struck by a large club in Kleatus's back arm.

"Are you okay, Kalvin?"

"I have a couple of bites, but they've stopped bleeding."

As they walked toward each other, they spotted Kitty. She carried Kandi in one arm and held a club in the other. She pushed toward them as fast as she could go.

"Eight creepers are behind us," she shouted. "Turn around and look behind you."

The other four creepers had stopped running, because a dozen more were coming through the forest to join them. Kleatus took Kandi and placed her in the large oak tree. Kandi stood on a large limb of the oak tree twenty-five feet from the ground. She held onto a branch with her back arms. In her right front arm tentacle she clutched a three-foot stick.

Kalvin and his parents backed up to the tree as they faced two dozen creepers.

CHAPTER FIFTEEN

༄

THE CREEPER BATTLE

The creepers in front of them and behind didn't attack. They just watched and waited.

"They may be waiting for more creepers to join them," said Kleatus. "Maybe we should charge them before they get here."

"No!" answered Kitty. "We'd have to leave Kandi unprotected in the tree."

"She's twenty-five feet above the ground," added Kalvin. "She's out of danger in the tree."

"We're staying here," stated Kitty. "The squirrels and forest animals are spreading the word about the creepers. Karl, Karen and Karrie are most likely headed toward us."

Several minutes later six more large creepers appeared on their right side.

"Told you," said Kleatus. "There are thirty of them now."

All the creepers slowly moved toward them.

"Get ready!" shouted Kleatus. "Here they come!"

The first to reach them were the eight behind them. The creepers began to wrap their tentacles around their feet and lower bodies. Kalvin and his parents smashed their clubs on the creepers and three more of them were dead. Other creepers wrapped tentacles around their clubs, but the little creatures were jerked into the air. A creeper hanging onto

Kitty's club was slung off and went sailing into the air. Two held onto Kleatus's massive club. He swung his club in an arc and slammed them into a tree. They fell to the ground and didn't move.

Kalvin and his parents had moved away from each other and away from the tree. They couldn't swing their clubs when they stood close together. Kalvin glanced back toward his sister and saw that she was hitting at two creepers that had climbed the tree. Two more were creeping up the tree behind her.

Oh, no, creepers can climb. I need to help Kandi before those other two grab her from behind.

Kalvin pushed toward Kandi as a creeper bit at one of his feet and another hung onto his lower left arm. Kalvin raised his left arm and battered the creeper hanging onto it with his club. The creeper dropped to the ground dead. Kalvin ignored the pain in his foot as he moved under Kandi.

"Kandi, jump to me," he shouted. "Two more are behind you."

Kandi jumped and Kalvin caught her in his upper arms as he beat at the creeper gnawing on his foot. Pain shot through his foot; the creature had bitten off the tip of his tentacle. His club smashed into the creeper. Green blood from his foot mingled with the creeper's black blood.

Another creeper bites the dust, Kalvin thought. *Kandi must weigh about a hundred and fifty pounds. I nearly dropped her. I'm free of creepers, but they're crawling all over Mom and Dad.*

Kalvin held Kandi in his upper left tentacle as he hurried to help his mom. Six creepers clung to her as she struggled to free herself. Three creepers moved toward Kalvin as he knocked one of the creatures off his mother's back.

He struck another that was chewing on one of her back arms as a creeper climbed up his back. The creeper started to bite his lower left arm when Kandi whacked it with her stick. The creeper hissed and climbed toward Kandi as she struck him a second blow.

"I can't hit him hard enough!" yelled Kandi. "He won't let go of you."

The other two creepers bit Kalvin's feet, but he continued to knock creepers off his mother.

"Ha," said Kandi. "I hit him in the eye and he dropped to the ground."

"Good job, Kandi, can you hit the ones on my feet?"

"You'll have to put me in a lower arm for me to reach them."

Kalvin lowered Kandi to his lower left arm tentacle as he smashed the last one on his mom's back. He looked toward his dad. Kleatus had a creeper in each of his large front tentacles. He stretched his arms wide and slammed the two creepers together. As he dropped the two stunned creatures, eight more continued to bite his arms and feet.

"Hitting them in the eye is working well," squealed Kandi as a creeper let go of Kalvin's foot.

Kandi began to beat at the other creeper and Kalvin knocked a creature off his dad's back. Green blood was dripping from all of them as the creepers continued to bite their arms and feet. Even Kandi had a cut across her arm. Eight creepers are dead and six others unconscious, but sixteen were still attacking them.

Kalvin heard a loud bellow as Karl and Karen waded into the fight. Karen threw rocks while Karl beat at them with clubs in his front three arms.

"Karrie is close behind," shouted Karen. "She doesn't move very fast; she's over ninety years old."

Some of the unconscious creepers began to wake up, but the tables had turned. There were now six kudzu monsters and four more creepers were dead. The creepers began to scatter. By the time Kalvin and his parents were free of creepers, fifteen of the creatures were dead. One creeper turned to run and was killed by Karrie coming up a hill. Kalvin handed Kandi to his mom and joined Kleatus and Karl as they chased after the fleeing creatures.

Karl threw one of his clubs to kill a fleeing creeper. Kalvin and Kleatus copied him and threw their clubs. The creepers kept fleeing and didn't turn to attack. Kalvin and his dad chased six of them and Karl pursued the others. Kleatus killed three more and Kalvin smashed another.

Four of the creatures had stopped fleeing and turned on Karl. He killed all of them, but had been bitten several times.

The three male monsters returned to where the females were after killing all but two of the creepers. Karrie was bandaging his mother's wounds. Kandi had her arm wrapped with something like a long green leaf.

"The last two creepers crawled into the lake," said Kleatus. "Maybe they'll drown."

"Creepers can breathe underwater," Karrie replied. "They'll stay underwater and feed on fish, frogs and snakes. Then they'll sneak away some night. Come over here and I'll bind your wounds."

No one was badly injured. Most of them were bleeding in several places. "We killed over thirty of them today," Karrie remarked. "They're gone for this year, but next year they'll be back in greater numbers. The creepers migrate through here every thirty or forty years and the third year of their migration is the worst. The horde queen that gives birth to them will be with them."

"How many creepers come with the queen?" asked Kalvin.

"There could be two hundred or more with her and two to four of her drones. I'll need all of you with me next year and with all the help you can bring."

Two hundred of them, Kalvin thought. *We had our hands full with three dozen.*

CHAPTER SIXTEEN

ᕦ

HOME AT LAST

That night all the kudzu monsters sat around talking about the battle with the creepers.

"Karrie," asked Kalvin, "how many creepers did you fight last year?"

"There were nine of them, Kalvin."

"You killed them all by yourself?"

"I had some help from a kudzu monster named Kokamo and some unexpected help. The creepers ran into a large pack of coyotes and they started fighting. Kokamo and I waited in the woods on opposite sides of the fight. If a creeper ran in my direction I clobbered it and Kokamo got the ones running in the other direction. I got two of them, the coyotes killed three and Kokamo polished off the others."

"How many kudzu monsters helped you thirty years ago against the two hundred creepers?" asked Kitty.

"There were eight of us," answered Karrie. "Kleatus, Karl and Karen were there and four others. A monster named Kanoe was badly injured."

"A man helped us, too," added Kleatus.

"Yes," added Karrie, "his name was Robert. He lived in a little cabin at the edge of the forest and had a shotgun with quite a lot of buckshot ammunition. He killed dozens of the critters. He was a great help, but he passed away some years ago."

"We probably won't have human help next year," said Karl.

"About seventy-five years ago we fought them for the first time," Karrie continued. "There were around a hundred and fifty creepers with the queen. Back then a lot more bears, wolves and cougars lived around here. They thinned out the creeper army quite a bit. Only a few bears are left now."

"What happened to the horde queen?" asked Kalvin.

"She was able to escape both times," answered Karrie. "If we could kill her, the attacks would stop, unless there's another creeper queen somewhere. But I doubt they would take the same route north."

Everyone stayed with Karrie for another week then headed back home. Kalvin and his family had a leisurely two-week journey.

"That was quite an adventure," said Kalvin. "I left in mid-October and returned home in early May."

"You were supposed to be gone a few weeks," answered Kitty.

"Well, it's behind us now," added Kleatus. "Let's just enjoy the peace and quiet of being back home."

"Hey, everybody," said a high-pitched voice in a tree. It was their squirrel friend, Squiggy.

"Squiggy, old buddy, it's good to see you again," answered Kalvin.

"I would like to introduce my daughter, Sparkle," announced Squiggy.

"I didn't know you had a family," said Kalvin.

"Well, she's an orphan. Lightning hit the tree she was living in and it caught fire. Sparkle jumped in a stream and ended up on a log in the middle of a lake. She was the only one who survived in the squirrel community. I saw her on the log and she's been with me ever since."

A small squirrel with a bushy tail that was bigger than her body peeked at them from behind Squiggy.

"Hi, Sparkle," Kandi greeted the timid little squirrel.

The little squirrel didn't say anything and quickly disappeared behind her new father.

"She's a little shy," said Squiggy. "Oh, by the way, go check out the family that moved into the house where your human friend Maranda used to live, Kandi."

"Kalvin, let's go see," exclaimed Kandi.

"I was afraid you'd say that," answered Kalvin. "Okay, let's go see who's moving into the neighborhood."

"Be careful," added Kitty. "We don't need any more excitement just now."

"We'll be careful," yelled Kandi as she hurried into the forest.

Kalvin and Kandi pushed slowly through the wooded area between the lake and the house where Maranda used to live. They froze perfectly still when they heard a human voice. Someone from a distance was shouting Kandi's name.

"Who could be calling my name?" asked Kandi.

"What human knows your name?" Kalvin asked back.

They pushed as fast as they could to the edge of the woods. Across the farm by the edge of the stream a human girl stood looking into the forest.

"It's Maranda," squealed Kandi. "She's come back."

Kandi hurried toward Maranda with Kalvin close behind.

I hope no unfriendly humans are about. Kandi didn't look around. She just started running.

"Maranda," shouted Kandi.

Maranda turned, hesitated, and then ran toward Kandi.

"Kandi, you've grown," said Maranda. "You're nearly as tall as me now."

"I'll be as tall as you by the end of summer. Then I'll only grow seven or eight inches a year for a few more years. After that my growth will slow down even more. What are you doing back here? Are you moving back into the house?"

"Yes," shouted Maranda. "My dad came back."

Where was your dad?" asked Kalvin.

"He was doing some construction work for a missionary overseas and he was captured by some bad men. They were holding him for ransom, but he was rescued by some soldiers."

"I don't understand all that you told me," answered Kandi. "But you can explain it to me sometime."

"Does your dad know about us?" asked Kalvin.

"Yes, but I'm not sure he believed us."

"He'll believe you when we knock on his door," answered Kalvin.

63

"Don't do that," Maranda quickly said. "Let me bring him to meet you. It'll take time for him to get used to kudzu monsters in the forest. But we'll have lots of time for him to adjust to you."

Maranda and Kandi stood there and smiled at each other. Kalvin's thoughts drifted back to the creepers they had fought. *I'm not going to worry about next year*, Kalvin said to himself. *I'm going to enjoy the spring and summer. This fall and winter we can start preparing for the creeper queen and her invading army.*

THE END